Suzy Mule

Barbara de
Illustrated by Eva Vagreti Cockrille

The Kane Press
New York

Cover Design: Sheryl Kagen

Library of Congress Cataloging-in-Publication Data

DeRubertis, Barbara.
Suzy Mule/Barbara deRubertis; illustrated by Eva Vagreti Cockrille.
p.   cm.
"A Let's read together book."

Summary: Suzy Mule follows her friend Bruce the Goose on his way south, and
when they arrive at Stu's Dude Ranch in the desert they decide to stay.
ISBN 1-57565-026-6 (pbk. : alk. paper)
[1. Mules--Fiction. 2. Geese--Fiction. 3. Stories in rhyme.]
I. Vagreti Cockrille, Eva, ill. II. Title.
PZ8.3.D455Su 1997   96-53889
[E]--dc21   CIP
                                                 AC

10 9 8 7 6 5 4

First published in the United States of America in 1997 by The Kane Press.
Printed in China.

LET'S READ TOGETHER is a registered trademark of The Kane Press.

Suzy Mule
has got the flu.
She sneezes twice.
"A-choo! A-choo!

"Brrr. It's cold.
   The wind is blowing.
   Brrr. Too cold.
   The snow is snowing."

Suzy hears
a honk. It's Bruce!
Suzy smiles.
It's Bruce the Goose!

5

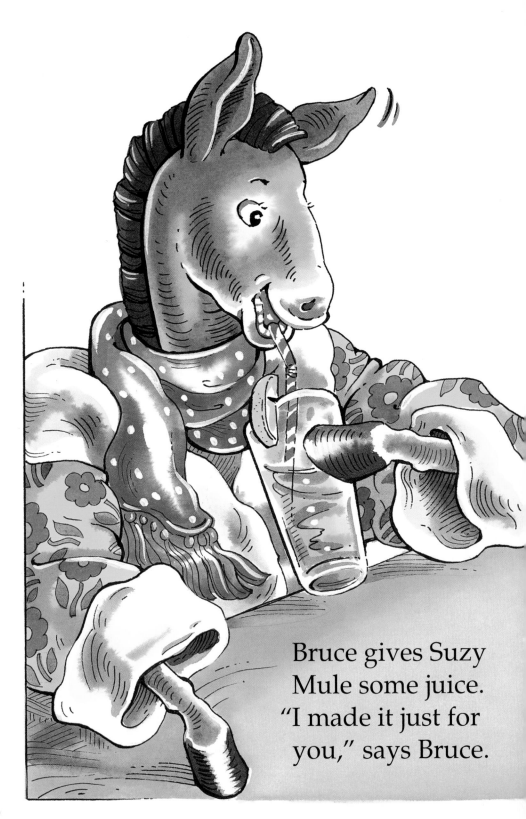

Bruce gives Suzy
Mule some juice.
"I made it just for
you," says Bruce.

Then he uses
lots of fruit
to make a funny
face. How cute!

Suzy thanks her good friend Bruce. What would she do without this goose?

Bruce says, "Suzy, I must go. Each winter, I fly south, you know."

Suzy says,
"I'll be like you.
I'll go south, too.
That's what I'll do."

"But mules can't fly!"
says Bruce the Goose.
"That's true," says Suzy
Mule to Bruce.

"So I must get a
truck to use.
Then you can fly.
And I can cruise!"

The friends set out.
One high. One low.
They both go south.
One fast. One slow.

Suzy drives through
sandy dunes.
She sings some country
music tunes.

Suzy smiles.
She's in the sun.
She's feeling great.
She's having fun.

But Suzy's truck now
stops. How cruel.
Suzy has run
out of fuel.

Look! It's Suzy's
lucky day.
An emu sheriff
comes her way.

The emu says,
"Well, howdy-do!
I have come to
rescue you.

"A little gas
    will get you down
    to Stu's Dude Ranch,
    this side of town.

"Stu will be
    of help to you.
    And you might be
    of help to Stu!"

Suzy turns on
Dude Ranch Trail.
She reads the sign.
"Dude Ranch for SALE."

Suzy says,
"I must find Stu.
Oh, there he is!
Yoo-hoo! Yoo-hoo!"

Suzy says,
"I'd like to stay."
Stu the Mule says,
"Come this way."

Suzy stops.
She looks at Stu.
"I see you have
too much to do.

"In fact, I think
that you could use
a partner here.
Please don't refuse!"

Stu the Mule says,
"Are you sure?"
"I'm sure," she says.
"The air is pure.

"The sun is warm.
The sky is blue.
I'm sure it's what
I want to do."

Now June is here.
The ranch looks new!
Suzy plays her
uke for Stu.

The moon is huge.
The shade is cool.
And look who's cooking
by the pool!

Suzy sings
a happy tune.
Three happy friends
beneath the moon!